# Marco's Run

# Marco's Run

**Wesley Cartier**

**Illustrated by Reynold Ruffins**

**Green Light Readers**
**Harcourt, Inc.**
Orlando   Austin   New York   San Diego   Toronto   London

It's time for a run in the park.

As I run, I think, I must be fast.
I wish I could run like . . .

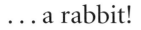. . . a rabbit!

A rabbit hops through the grass.
He's kicking with his long back legs.
Off he goes.

I run like that rabbit. I hop and kick.

Then I think, I must be fast.
I wish I could run like . . .

. . . a bobcat!

A bobcat runs on the forest path.
She darts off in a flash to hunt.

I run like that bobcat. I rush down
the park path.

Then I think, I must be very fast.
I wish I could run like . . .

. . . a horse!

A horse starts with a trot. Then, all of a sudden, she takes off like the wind!

I run like that horse. The wind
swishes past me.

Then I think, I must be the fastest of all.
I wish I could run like . . .

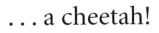. . . a cheetah!

A swift cheetah flashes by.
No one can catch him!

I run like that cheetah.

Then, I am huffing and puffing! I can't run anymore. Now I wish I were . . .

. . . back home.

I huff and puff and
sit down with a *thump*.

# Then I think . . .

NOW I NEED A REST!

# Animal Relay Races

**Marco pretends to be a rabbit, a bobcat,
a horse, and a cheetah.
Now you and your friends can act like
all these animals in a relay race!**

**1.** Line up in teams of four people.

**2.** The first person hops like a rabbit to
the finish line and back.

**3.** The second person crawls like a bobcat.

**4.** The third person trots like a horse.

**5.** The fourth person runs like a cheetah.

**When everyone is finished,
you can REST just like Marco!**

# ANIMAL MASKS

Make a mask of your favorite animal!

**Popsicle stick**

**crayons or markers**

**scissors**

## WHAT YOU'LL NEED

**paper plate**

**colored paper**

**tape**

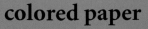
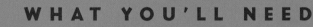

**1.** Draw the animal face on a paper plate. Use the colored paper to make ears, whiskers, and a nose.

**2.** Cut out holes for the eyes.

**3.** Tape a Popsicle stick to your mask.

**4.** Wear your mask. Tell a friend what you know about your animal.

# Meet the Illustrator

Reynold Ruffins loves to draw. He says, "Drawing can be a great adventure!" Drawing gives him the chance to show things that no one has ever thought of. "I like to show that pictures can tell a story just the way words do," he says.

*Reynold Ruffins*

Requests for permission to make copies of any part of the work should be mailed
to the following address: Permissions Department, Harcourt, Inc.,
6277 Sea Harbor Drive, Orlando, Florida 32887-6777.

www.HarcourtBooks.com

First Green Light Readers edition 2001
*Green Light Readers* is a trademark of Harcourt, Inc., registered in the
United States of America and/or other jurisdictions.

The Library of Congress has cataloged an earlier edition as follows:
Cartier, Wesley.
Marco's run/by Wesley Cartier; illustrated by Reynold Ruffins.
p. cm.
"Green Light Readers."
Summary: A boy runs so fast that he imagines himself to be a rabbit, a bobcat, a
horse, and a cheetah.
[1. Running—Fiction.  2. Speed—Fiction.  3. Imagination—Fiction.
4. Animals—Fiction.]  I. Ruffins, Reynold, ill.  II. Title.  III. Green Light reader.
PZ7.C2485Mar  2001
[E]—dc21    00-9727
ISBN 0-15-204868-5
ISBN 0-15-204828-6 (pb)

A C E G H F D B
A C E G H F D B (pb)

**Ages 5–7**
**Grades: 1–2**
**Guided Reading Level: G–H**
**Reading Recovery Level: 14–15**

## Green Light Readers
### For the reader who's ready to GO!

"A must-have for any family with a beginning reader."—*Boston Sunday Herald*

"You can't go wrong with adding several copies of these terrific books to your beginning-to-read collection."—*School Library Journal*

"A winner for the beginner."—*Booklist*

## Five Tips to Help Your Child Become a Great Reader

**1.** Get involved. Reading aloud to and with your child is just as important as encouraging your child to read independently.

**2.** Be curious. Ask questions about what your child is reading.

**3.** Make reading fun. Allow your child to pick books on subjects that interest her or him.

**4.** Words are everywhere—not just in books. Practice reading signs, packages, and cereal boxes with your child.

**5.** Set a good example. Make sure your child sees YOU reading.

## Why Green Light Readers Is the Best Series for Your New Reader

● Created exclusively for beginning readers by some of the biggest and brightest names in children's books

● Reinforces the reading skills your child is learning in school

● Encourages children to read—and finish—books by themselves

● Offers extra enrichment through fun, age-appropriate activities unique to each story

● Incorporates characteristics of the Reading Recovery program used by educators

● Developed with Harcourt School Publishers and credentialed educational consultants

**Daniel's Mystery Egg**
Alma Flor Ada/G. Brian Karas

**A Bed Full of Cats**
Holly Keller

**Animals on the Go**
Jessica Brett/Richard Cowdrey

**The Fox and the Stork**
Gerald McDermott

**Marco's Run**
Wesley Cartier/Reynold Ruffins

**Boots for Beth**
Alex Moran/Lisa Campbell Ernst

**Digger Pig and the Turnip**
Caron Lee Cohen/Christopher Denise

**Catch Me If You Can!**
Bernard Most

**Tumbleweed Stew**
Susan Stevens Crummel/Janet Stevens

**The Very Boastful Kangaroo**
Bernard Most

**The Chick That Wouldn't Hatch**
Claire Daniel/Lisa Campbell Ernst

**Farmers Market**
Carmen Parks/Edward Martinez

**Splash!**
Ariane Dewey/Jose Aruego

**Shoe Town**
Janet Stevens/Susan Stevens Crummel

**Get That Pest!**
Erin Douglas/Wong Herbert Yee

**The Enormous Turnip**
Alexei Tolstoy/Scott Goto

**Why the Frog Has Big Eyes**
Betsy Franco/Joung Un Kim

**Where Do Frogs Come From?**
Alex Vern

**I Wonder**
Tana Hoban

**The Purple Snerd**
Rozanne Lanczak Williams/
Mary GrandPré

**Look for more Green Light Readers wherever books are sold!**